Puzzle Maps
U.S.A.

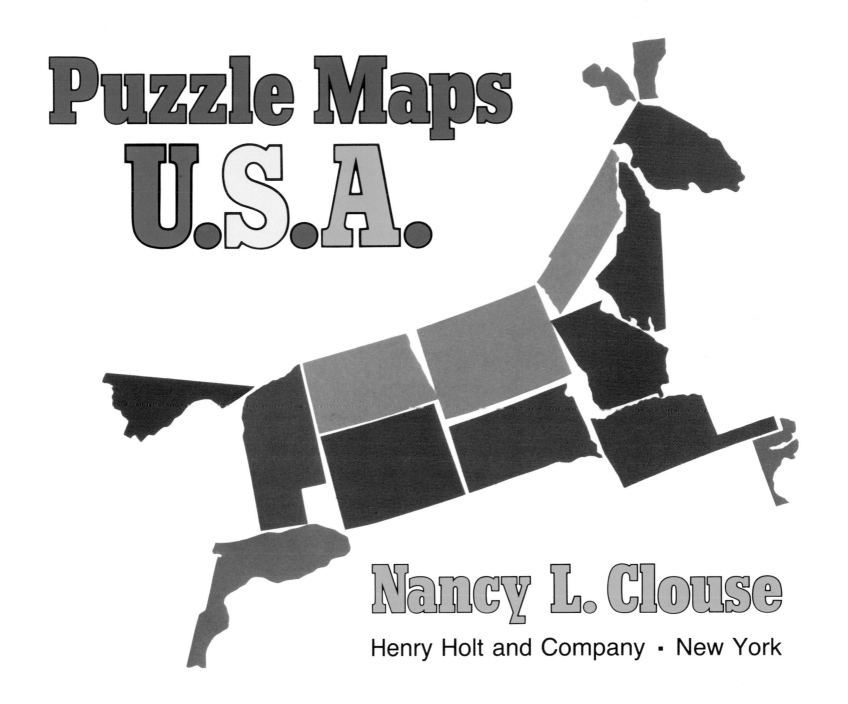

Puzzle Maps U.S.A.

U.S.A.

Nancy L. Clouse

Henry Holt and Company · New York

In memory of Mary Jane Anway—
artist, educator, and friend

Henry Holt and Company, Inc.
Publishers since 1866
115 West 18th Street
New York, New York 10011

Henry Holt is a registered
trademark of Henry Holt and Company, Inc.

Published in Canada by Fitzhenry & Whiteside Ltd.,
195 Allstate Parkway, Markham, Ontario L3R 4T8.

Library of Congress Cataloging-in-Publication Data
Clouse, Nancy L.
Puzzle maps U.S.A. / Nancy L. Clouse
Summary: Introduces the fifty states and their shapes through a
series of simple puzzle maps.
1. United States—Geography—Juvenile literature.   2. United
States—Maps—Juvenile literature.   3. Children's questions
and answers.   4. Puzzles—Juvenile literature.   [1. United States—
Maps.   2. Puzzles.]   I. Title.
E161.3.C46   1990
912.73—dc20   89-24604

ISBN 0-8050-1143-9 (hardcover)
10   9   8   7   6   5   4   3   2
ISBN 0-8050-3597-4 (paperback)
10   9   8   7   6   5   4   3   2

First published in hardcover in 1990 by Henry Holt and Company, Inc.
First Owlet edition, 1994

Printed in Mexico

Maps can be a lot of fun!

Alaska*

PACIFIC OCEAN

MEXICO

Here is a map of the United States.

There are 50 states in all.
Can you find the state where you live?

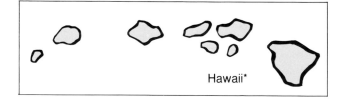

Hawaii*

*Not to scale

CANADA

North Dakota

Minnesota

Michigan

New Hampshire

Vermont

Maine

South Dakota

Wisconsin

New York

Iowa

Massachusetts

Rhode Island

Nebraska

Pennsylvania

Connecticut

New Jersey

Kansas

Illinois

Indiana

Ohio

Delaware

Maryland

Missouri

West Virginia

Virginia

District of Columbia

Kentucky

Oklahoma

Arkansas

Tennessee

North Carolina

South Carolina

Alabama

Georgia

ATLANTIC OCEAN

Texas

Mississippi

Louisiana

Florida

GULF OF MEXICO

This is a puzzle map of the United States.
It can be taken apart and put back together.

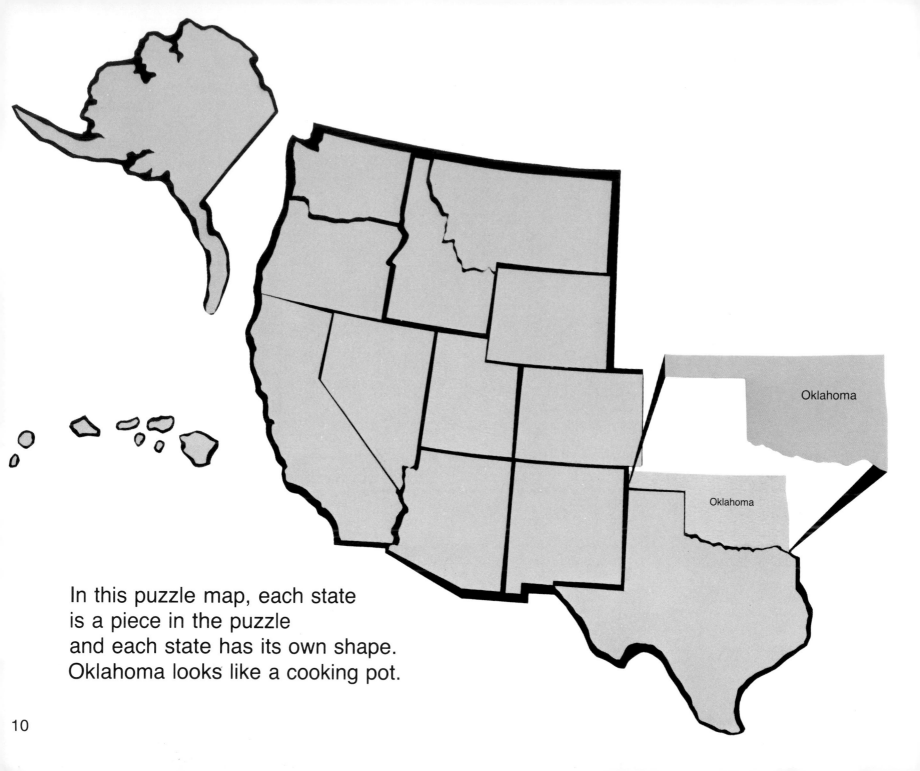

In this puzzle map, each state
is a piece in the puzzle
and each state has its own shape.
Oklahoma looks like a cooking pot.

Michigan looks like a mitten with a scarf.

Louisiana looks like an armchair with a fringe.

Florida looks like a boomerang or a boot.

What does your state look like?

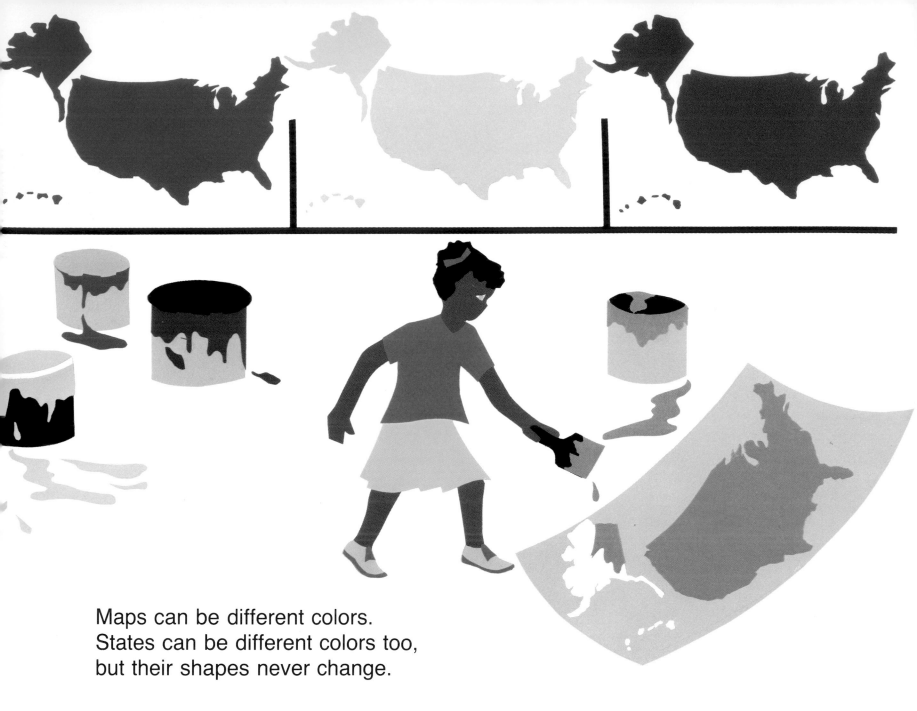

Maps can be different colors.
States can be different colors too,
but their shapes never change.

There are ten puzzle pieces on this page, but only three states.
Colorado looks like a box. How many times do you see Colorado?
California looks like an arm bent at the elbow. How many times
do you see California?
South Carolina looks like a funny triangle. How many times
do you see South Carolina?

FLY U.S.A.

UNITED TRUCKING CO.

Maps on buildings and billboards
are very large.
Maps in books are small.
If a map of the U.S.A. is big,
then the states on that map will
be big too. If a map is small,
the states will be small too.

In this picture some states are big and some are small.
Is your state one of the kites flying high in the sky?

Maine, Nevada, New Mexico

These puzzle shapes are hard to juggle,

but you can still recognize their shapes
and name them.

Idaho, Utah, Wisconsin

17

Here's a picture-puzzle wagon. When you pull it,
Utah, Kansas, New Mexico, and Oklahoma go for a ride.

This turtle is going for a swim. Which states are going to get wet? The turtle's eye is the smallest state in the United States. Look closely at the turtle and you will find eight states in all.

Alabama, Connecticut, Kansas, Kentucky, Missouri, Nebraska, Oklahoma, Rhode Island

This funny bird wishes he could fly. Virginia and North Carolina are hiding in his bill. How many other states are in his feathers?

Alaska, Connecticut, Indiana, Kentucky, North Carolina, South Carolina, Texas, Virginia, West Virginia

This is a tree you'd never find in the park. Its trunk is made from Georgia, Mississippi, and Alabama. Which states are in the leaves?

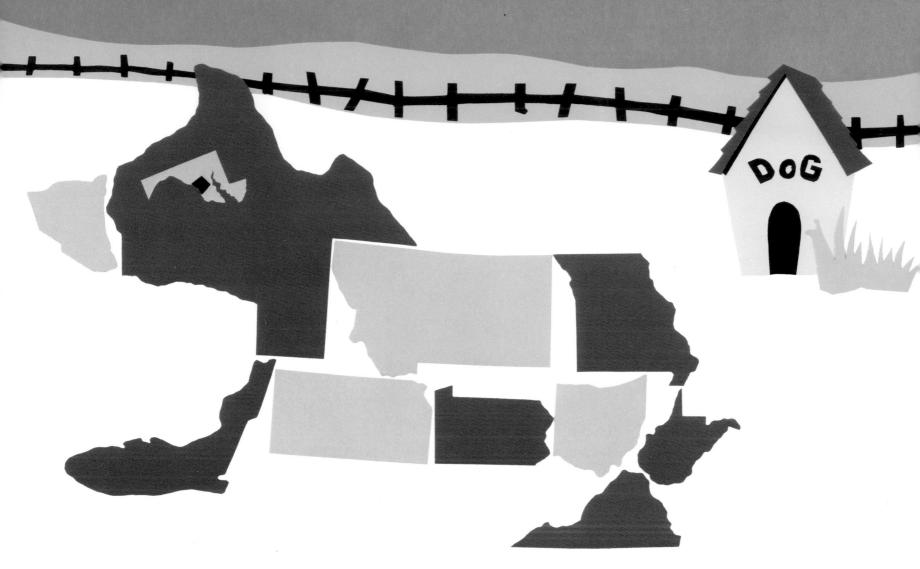

Does this spotted dog have a tail to wag? You can see the capital of the United States in his eye. What is it?
How many states can you find?

Here is a pretty flower growing in a pot. Is your state here? Is it in the blossom, the stem, or the flowerpot?

Alabama, California, Idaho, Illinois, Iowa, Kentucky, Louisiana, New York, North Carolina, Ohio, Oregon, Tennessee, Washington

Is your state going for a walk with this man and his dog?

Round and round goes this carousel horse. Is your state bobbing up and down on the merry-go-round?

Colorado, Florida, Georgia, Illinois, Indiana, Kentucky, Maryland, Nebraska, New Jersey, North Carolina, North Dakota, Oklahoma, South Dakota, Tennessee, Vermont, Wyoming

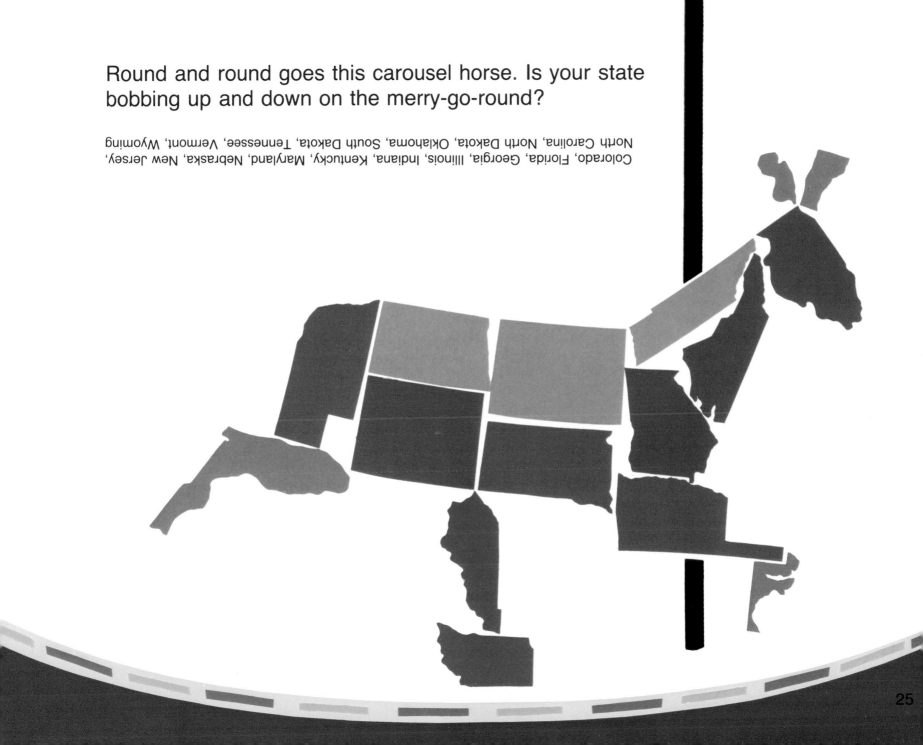

This clown works at the circus. Is your state there with him?
Which states are there?

Alaska, Arizona, Arkansas, California, Connecticut, Delaware, Hawaii, Idaho, Louisiana, Maine, Massachusetts, Michigan, Minnesota, Mississippi, Missouri, Montana, Nevada, New Hampshire, New Mexico, Oregon, Rhode Island, South Carolina, Utah, Virginia, West Virginia, Wisconsin

Trivia U.S.A.

1. East of the Mississippi River, which state is the largest?
2. Which state is the smallest in the U.S.A.?
3. The Mississippi River begins in what state?
4. Which state is the largest in the U.S.A.?
5. Where can you stand on four states all at once?
6. Which five states have beaches on the Gulf of Mexico?
7. Which five states have land touching the Pacific Ocean?
8. How many states touch the border of our southern neighbor, Mexico? Can you name them?
9. Which fourteen states are on the Atlantic Ocean?
10. The Mississippi River enters the Gulf of Mexico through which state?
11. Which thirteen states share a land or water border with our northern neighbor, Canada?
12. Which state has two parts, a lower peninsula and an upper peninsula?
13. The capital of the United States, the District of Columbia, is also known as Washington, D.C. Which two states does it border?

Puzzle Keys

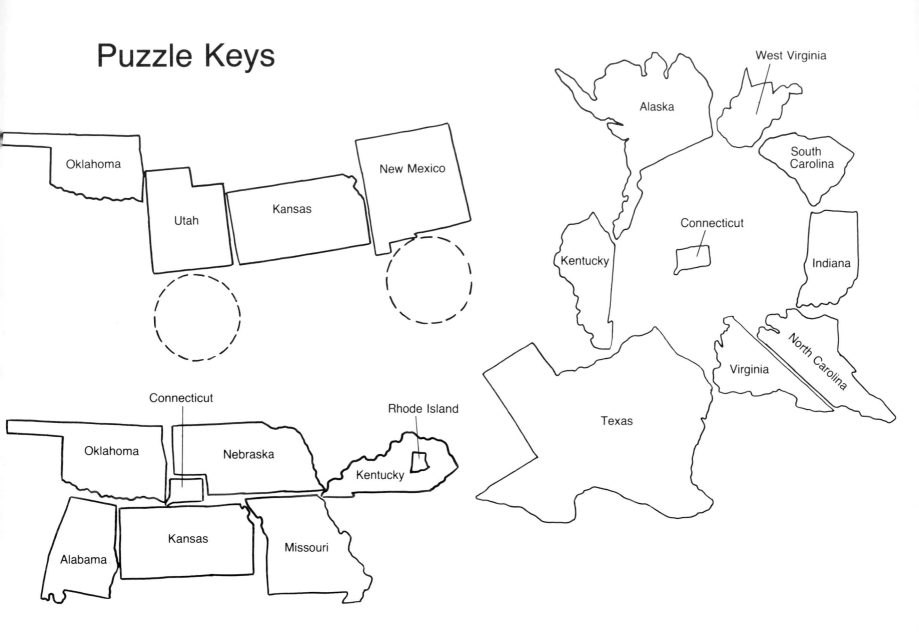

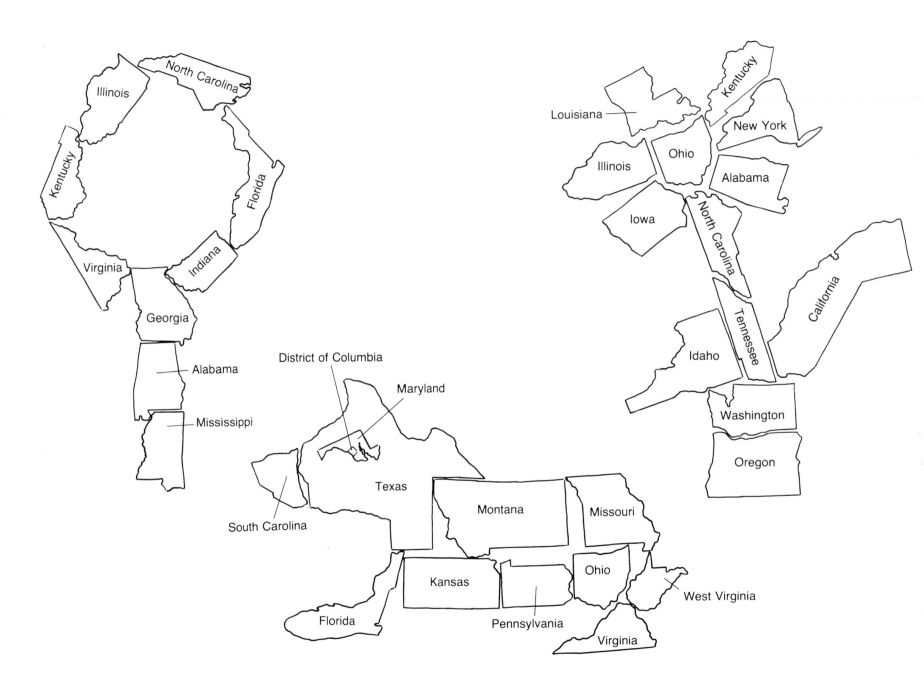

North Carolina

Illinois

Kentucky

Florida

Virginia

Indiana

Georgia

Alabama

Mississippi

Louisiana

Kentucky

New York

Illinois

Ohio

Alabama

Iowa

North Carolina

California

Tennessee

Idaho

Washington

Oregon

District of Columbia

Maryland

Texas

South Carolina

Montana

Missouri

Florida

Kansas

Ohio

West Virginia

Pennsylvania

Virginia

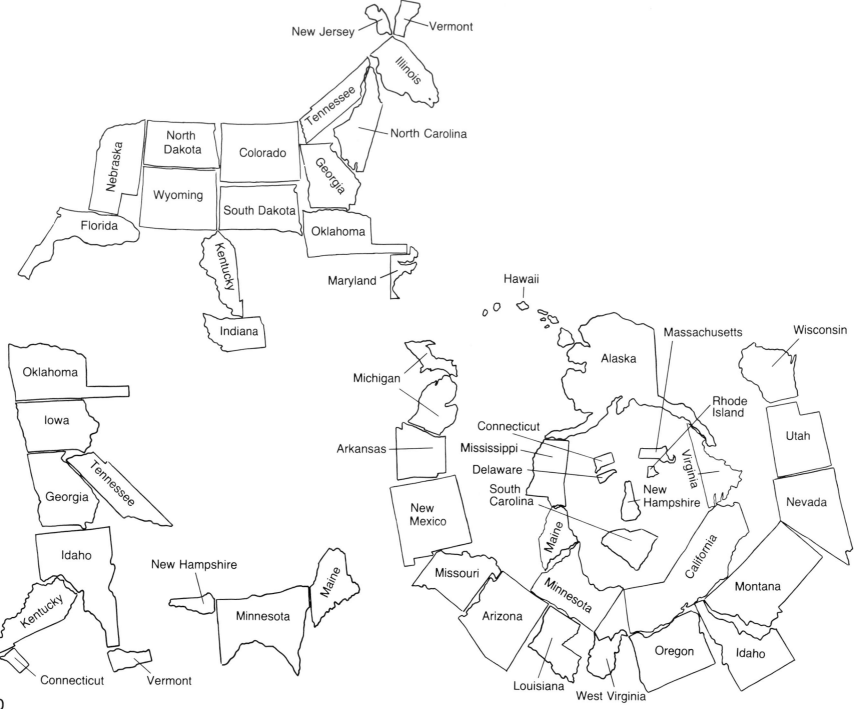

New Jersey — Vermont

Illinois

Tennessee

North Carolina

Nebraska

North Dakota

Colorado

Georgia

Wyoming

South Dakota

Oklahoma

Florida

Kentucky

Maryland

Indiana

Hawaii

Massachusetts

Wisconsin

Alaska

Oklahoma

Michigan

Rhode Island

Iowa

Connecticut

Mississippi

Virginia

Utah

Tennessee

Arkansas

Delaware

Georgia

South Carolina

New Hampshire

Nevada

Idaho

New Mexico

Maine

New Hampshire

Missouri

Minnesota

Montana

Kentucky

Minnesota

Arizona

California

Connecticut

Vermont

Louisiana

West Virginia

Oregon

Idaho

30

Trivia U.S.A.—Answers

1. Georgia.
2. Rhode Island.
3. Minnesota.
4. Alaska. It is so large that if a map of it were drawn to the same scale as the maps of the other states, it would be almost as big as all the other states put together.
5. Arizona, Colorado, New Mexico, Utah.
6. Alabama, Florida, Louisiana, Mississippi, Texas.
7. Alaska, California, Hawaii, Oregon, Washington.
8. Four states: Arizona, California, New Mexico, Texas.
9. Connecticut, Delaware, Florida, Georgia, Maine, Maryland, Massachusetts, New Hampshire, New Jersey, New York, North Carolina, Rhode Island, South Carolina, Virginia.
10. Louisiana
11. Alaska, Idaho, Maine, Michigan, Minnesota, Montana, North Dakota, New Hampshire, New York, Ohio, Pennsylvania, Vermont, Washington.
12. Michigan.
13. Maryland and Virginia.

Index